A Tale of Two Cities

Charles Dickens

Adapted by Nigel Flynn

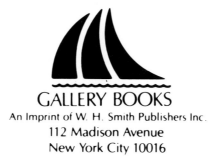

GALLERY BOOKS
An Imprint of W. H. Smith Publishers Inc.
112 Madison Avenue
New York City 10016

This book was devised and produced by
Multimedia Publications (UK) Ltd.

Editor: Nigel Flynn (Acorn Press)
Designer: Janette Place
Production: Arnon Orbach

First published in the United States of America 1985 by
Gallery Books, an imprint of W. H. Smith Publishers Inc.,
112 Madison Avenue, New York, NY 10016

ISBN 0 8317 8625 6

Typeset by Waveney Typesetters, Norwich, Norfolk
Origination by DS Colour International Ltd., London
Printed in Italy by Amilcare Pizzi SpA., Milan

Contents

The Life of Charles Dickens

Charles John Huffham Dickens was born on 7 February 1812, in the English coastal town of Portsmouth, where his father, John Dickens, was a clerk in the Navy Pay Office. John Dickens was 26 when Charles was born and was an excitable, extravagant man who liked to entertain in style — a style that his meagre salary as a clerk was unable to support. This was to lead him into a succession of financial crises throughout his life.

The second of eight children, Charles was a delicate, sensitive child, unable to join in the play of other children, and he withdrew into books. Later in life, recalling his boyhood days, he wrote: "When I think of it, the picture always arises in my mind of a summer evening, the boys at play in the churchyard and I sitting on my bed, reading as if for life."

The books that he read, introduced to him by his father — books such as *Robinson Crusoe*, *The Arabian Nights*, *Don Quixote* and a child's *Tom Jones* — created for him a world of magic, wonder and adventure, a world that he himself was so vividly to create for others to enjoy in his own books.

At the age of 12 the childhood of Dickens came to a sudden and dramatic end. His father, unable to pay his large debts, was packed off to the Marshalsea Debtors' Prison in London. Within a few days the rest of the family were to join him there — all, that is, except Charles, whose education was cut short and who was made to earn his living, washing bottles, at Warren's Blacking Factory. This experience proved so shocking and humiliating to the boy that it was to haunt him for the rest of his life. "No words can express the secret agony of my soul . . . I felt my early hopes of growing up to be a learned and distinguished man crushed in my breast."

Though soon re-united with his family, the previous easy life enjoyed by Charles was never to return. Two years later, at the age of 14, his irregular and inadequate schooling ended and he began work as a clerk in a lawyer's office in Gray's Inn, London. This experience, again not a happy one, gave him two things — a lifelong loathing of the legal profession and much raw material for many of his later novels.

Dickens then became a reporter on the parliamentary newspaper *True Sun*, where his natural talent for reporting and keen observation was first recognized. He taught himself shorthand and, on the *Mirror of Parliament*, and then the *Morning Chronicle*, he was soon acknowledged as the best parliamentary reporter of the age.

In 1833, now very much the young man about town, Dickens wrote his first piece of fiction: *A Dinner at Poplar Walk*, in the *Old Monthly Magazine*. Asked by the editor to contribute more, under the pen name 'Boz', Dickens wrote a series of pieces that were collected and published in 1836 under the title *Sketches by Boz*.

The modest success of *Sketches* was followed by the enormously popular and successful *Pickwick Papers*, which was published in monthly instalments in 1836 and 1837. Pickwick became a national hero overnight, and his exploits were followed by an average of 40,000 readers. Though not yet 30, Dickens was now rich and famous.

Two days after the publication of Pickwick, Dickens married Catherine Hogarth, daughter of a fellow journalist. "So perfect a creature never breathed," he wrote of her at the time, "she had not a fault." But with time his view of her was to change, and in later years he was to admit, "She is amiable and complying but nothing on earth would make her understand me." They were to separate in 1858, when Dickens was 46.

Throughout his life Dickens enjoyed travelling. In the 1840s he journeyed to Scotland, America, France, Switzerland and Italy. And throughout this period he poured out a succession of novels that exposed the cruelty, hypocrisy and appalling poverty of early Victorian society, novels such as *Oliver Twist*, *Nicholas Nickleby*, *The Old Curiosity Shop*, *Barnaby Rudge*, *A Christmas Carol*, *Martin Chuzzlewit*, and *Dombey and Son*.

Even his novel writing (which continued to be published in monthly instalments) proved inadequate for his boundless energy and restless spirit. In the 1840s, apart from all his major novels, and work on *David Copperfield* (published in 1850), he started a daily newspaper, the *Daily News*, and a weekly magazine, *Household Words*, in addition to writing a travel book *American Notes* and a three-volume *Child's History of England*.

In all that he wrote Dickens strove to draw people together and lead them to a better understanding of each other. As he himself believed, "In this world a great deal of bitterness among us arises from an imperfect understanding of one another."

But as he grew older, the subjects he wrote of grew bleaker and the mood more grim. *Bleak House, Hard Times, Little Dorrit, A Tale of Two Cities, Great Expectations, Our Mutual Friend* and his unfinished novel, *The Mystery of Edwin Drood*, all reflect a growing pessimism.

Despite a steady decline in health, Dickens continued to give dramatic public readings of his works to packed houses in both Britain and the United States, which he visited again in 1867–68. Of these a contemporary witness reported, "He seemed to be physically transformed as he passed from one character to another; he had as many distinct voices as his books had characters; he held at command the fountains of laughter and tears . . . When he sat down it was not mere applause that followed, but a passionate outburst of love for the man."

But the strain proved too much and on 8 June 1870, during a farewell series of talks in England, he suffered a stroke, and the next day he died at his home, Gad's Hill Place, near Rochester, Kent, at the age of 58.

Two days after his death Queen Victoria wrote in her diary, "He is a very great loss. He had a large loving mind and the strongest sympathy with the poorer classes." On 14 June he was buried in Poet's Corner, Westminster Abbey, close to the monuments of Chaucer and Shakespeare.

Charles Dickens in his study at Gad's Hill Place, his home near Rochester, Kent, reproduced by kind permission of the Trustees of the Dickens House (*Dickens' Dream* by R. W. Buss)

Introduction

THE two cities of Dickens' title are Paris and London in the time of the French Revolution. This event, one of the most far-reaching in European history, began with the storming of the Bastille prison on the morning of 14 July, 1789.

When Charles Dickens came to write his story he asked the famous historian Thomas Carlyle what books he should read in order to acquaint himself with the background to the French Revolution. In response, Carlyle had two cartloads of books delivered to Dickens' home. Sensibly, Dickens read none of them; instead he read Carlyle's own book *The French Revolution*. The story he then wrote, although set at the time of the Revolution, is a dramatic tale of passion, cruelty, intrigue, love and terror.

Dickens loathed political injustice. As he told a slave owner during one of his visits to America, "Cruelty and the abuse of absolute power are two of the bad passions of human nature." Cruelty and the abuse of power are the two great themes of *A Tale of Two Cities*. The miserable wretches who live in the squalid backstreets of Paris before the Revolution suffer because men like the Marquis St Evrémonde abuse their power. Dickens then shows us the other side of the coin: when pent-up vengeance and hatred are released, as they were in France in the years following the Revolution, one tyranny is replaced by another — tyranny by the aristocracy is replaced by tyranny by the mob.

Although great historical events echo through the pages of *A Tale of Two Cities* the centre of the stage is held by ordinary folk intent upon the ordinary business of living. To Dickens, history is made by individuals. The fear that chills Lucie Manette when she hears the fall of footsteps outside her father's house in London is a fear felt by many: that those they love will be taken away from them and that the life they lead, happily and quietly, will be destroyed.

As he unfolds his story, Dickens shows us another great truth: that while great events — wars and revolutions — destroy and crush some people, they also summon up nobility and courage in others. Sydney Carton, drunk, aimless and morose, gives his life so that the friends he loves can live happily. He is the real hero of the story.

Dickens' portrayal of Paris during the Revolution is an imaginative masterpiece. A Londoner at heart, Dickens nevertheless carries us back convincingly and vividly to the streets of Paris during the days of the Terror, days made more terrible by the menacing Madame Defarge and the presence of the guillotine.

As in all Dickens' books, there are many minor characters who are essential to the plot; Jerry Cruncher is a good example — he makes possible the self-sacrifice of Sydney Carton and the escape of Charles Darnay. In a world that has taken leave of its senses, only the calm and reasonable Mr Jarvis Lorry seems sane.

First published in 1859, *A Tale of Two Cities* soon became as popular as *Oliver Twist*. Even today, many people who have never read *A Tale of Two Cities* know the immortal words spoken by Sydney Carton moments before his death, "It is a far, far better thing that I do, than I have ever done . . .".

1 Recalled to Life

It was the best of times, it was the worst of times; it was the age of wisdom, it was the age of foolishness. It was the year 1775.

On a Friday night late in November, a stage-coach was struggling through thick mud up Shooter's Hill on its way to Dover, when a horse came fast and furious through the fog.

"So-ho!" cried out the guard as loud as he could roar. "Yo there! Stand or I'll fire!"

"Is that the Dover Mail?"

"Why do you want to know?"

"I want a passenger, if it is."

"What passenger?"

"Mr Jarvis Lorry of Tellson's bank."

"Keep where you are," the guard called to the voice in the mist. "If I should make a mistake, it could never be set right in your lifetime. Gentleman of the name of Lorry answer straight."

"What's the matter?" asked a passenger. "Who wants me? Is it you, Jerry?"

"Yes, Mr Lorry," answered the voice.

"I know this messenger, guard," said Mr Lorry, opening the door. "He may come close."

The figures of a horse and rider came slowly through the mist to the side of the coach where Mr Lorry stood. The rider stooped, and casting his eye up at the guard, handed the passenger a small folded paper.

Mr Lorry opened it in the light of the coach-lamp and read — first to himself and then aloud: '*Wait at Dover for Mam'selle.*' Then, pausing a moment, he said, "Jerry, say that my answer was RECALLED TO LIFE."

"That's a blazing strange answer," said Jerry.

"Take that message back, and they will know that I received this. Now hurry back. Goodnight."

With those words Mr Lorry opened the coach-door and got in. The coach lumbered on again, heavy wreaths of mist closing all around it. When eventually the coach arrived at the Royal George Hotel in Dover, Mr Lorry booked a room and said to the porter, "I wish

accommodation for a young lady who may come here at any time today. She may ask for Mr Jarvis Lorry, or she may ask for a gentleman from Tellson's bank. Let me know, immediately."

"Yes, sir."

Having eaten a good dinner, Mr Lorry sat drinking the last of his claret when he heard a rattling of wheels outside. A few minutes later the waiter came in to announce that Miss Manette had arrived from London, and would be happy to see the gentleman from Tellson's.

Mr Lorry emptied his glass, adjusted his wig and followed the waiter to Miss Manette's room.

"Pray take a seat, sir," said a slight young lady of not more than seventeen.

"I kiss your hand, miss," said Mr Lorry, as he made a formal bow and took his seat.

"I received a letter from the bank, sir," continued Miss Manette in a clear pleasant voice, a little foreign in accent, "informing me that some discovery respecting the small property of my poor father, whom I never saw and so long dead, rendered it necessary that I should go to Dover, there to communicate with a gentleman of the bank."

"Myself," replied Mr Lorry. "I was happy to be entrusted with the charge. I shall be more happy to execute it."

"Sir, I thank you indeed. I was told by the bank that the gentleman would explain to me the details of the business, and that I must prepare myself to find them of a surprising nature. I have done my best to prepare myself, and am curious to know what they are."

"Naturally, yes — I —." After a pause, Mr Lorry, after again settling his wig, continued, "it is very difficult to begin. I am a man of business. You know that your parents had no great possessions and that what they had was secured to your mother and to you. And that when your mother died, when you were just two years old, that it was I who brought you to England, a ward of Tellson's bank.

"That I know, sir."

"Well, Miss Manette, there has been no new discovery of money, or any other property. But — he has been found! Your father is still alive! Greatly changed, I fear, but still alive. For the last eighteen years he has been locked up in the dreaded Bastille prison. Now released, he has been taken to the house of an old servant — a Monsieur Defarge, now the owner of a wine-shop in Paris. Miss Manette, we are going there; we are going to Monsieur Defarge's wine-shop; I to identify your father, you to restore him to life.

A shiver ran through her frame. Then, in an instant, she slumped back in her chair, clutching Mr Lorry's hand.

"Miss Manette! *Miss Manette!* Whatever is the matter?" Just then a woman came running into the room. Seeing Mr Lorry, she said, "Don't just stand there! Bring smelling-salts, cold water and vinegar, quick!"

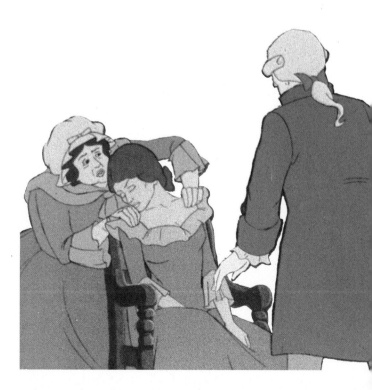

Mr Lorry did as he was told, while the woman picked Miss Manette up and laid her on the sofa.

"I hope she is feeling better now," said Mr Lorry when he returned.

"No thanks to you," replied the woman, who sat stroking Miss Manette's hair and calling her "my precious!" and "my bird!".

"I hope," said Mr Lorry, "that you will accompany Miss Manette and I to France?"

"If it was ever intended" said the woman, who was introduced to Mr Lorry as Miss Pross, "that I should go across salt water, why do you suppose I was born on an island?"

This being a question hard to answer, Mr Lorry withdrew.

Monsieur Defarge's wine-shop was in the district of Saint Antoine, the poorest part of Paris. The wine-shop was more prosperous than most of the houses of Saint Antoine, and its owner, Monsieur Defarge, better looking and stronger than most of the inhabitants.

Inside the shop, Madame Defarge sat knitting. She was a stout woman with strong features and a watchful eye. Her husband stood at the counter of the little shop when Mr Lorry and Miss Manette entered.

"A word, Monsieur Defarge," said Mr Lorry, when he had ordered some refreshment.

"Willingly, sir," said Defarge. Their conversation was short, and in less than a minute, Defarge nodded and went out. Mr Lorry beckoned to Miss Manette, then they followed Defarge through a stinking court-yard to a gloomy staircase.

"It's very high and difficult. You'd better go slowly," he said in a stern voice.

"Is he alone?" whispered Mr Lorry.

"Alone! Of course he's alone. Who should be with him?"

Mr Lorry's spirits grew heavier and heavier as they climbed higher and higher. At last, reaching the top, they stopped. Carefully feeling in the pockets of his trousers, Defarge took out a key.

"The door is locked, then, my friend?" asked Mr Lorry, "why?"

"Because he's lived so long, locked up, that he would be frightened — come to I know not what harm — if his door was left open."

"Is it possible?"

"Yes. And a beautiful world we live in, when it *is* possible, and when many other such things are possible, and not only possible, but done — done under that sky there, every day. Long live the Devil. Let us go in!"

The door slowly opened inward under his hand, and looking into the room, then back over his shoulder, Defarge beckoned the visitors to enter. The garret was dim and dark, and such a scanty portion of light was admitted that it was difficult to see anything. Gradually their eyes grew accustomed to the lack of light and they saw a white-haired man sitting on a low bench, stooping forward and making a pair of shoes.

"Good day!" said Defarge.

"Good day!" a faint voice responded, as if it was a long way off.

"You have a visitor."

"What did you say?"

"I said you have a visitor."

Mr Lorry stepped forward and picking up one of the shoes lying on the bench said, "May I ask what kind of shoe it is?"

"A lady's shoe," came the hesitant reply. "A young lady's walking-shoe."

"And may I inquire the maker's name?"

There was a long pause. The task of recalling

his name seemed too much for the white-haired man. "Did you ask my name?" he said, finally.

"I did."

"One Hundred and Five, North Tower."

"Is that all?"

"One Hundred and Five, North Tower." And with a weary sound that was not a sigh, nor a groan, he went back to work on his shoes.

"Monsieur Manette, do you remember nothing of me?" asked Mr Lorry, looking him full in the face. "Look at me. Do you not recognize me?"

The shoe dropped to the ground, and the man sat looking at Mr Lorry, blankly.

Not a word was spoken, not a sound was made. Like a spirit, Miss Manette moved and stood beside the man bent over his work. She put her two hands to her lips and kissed them to him.

"You are not the gaoler's daughter?"

"No," she sighed.

"Who are you?"

"Good sir, do you not know your name is Manette, the same name I bear?"

She held him closer and rocked him like a child. "My dear," she said, "Your agony is over. We've come to take you from it. We are going to England where you will be at peace and at rest."

Raising her hand to Mr Lorry, she said, "Would you make arrangements for our return to England at once?"

"If you think he's fit for the journey," said Mr Lorry.

"More fit for that," answered Monsieur Defarge, "than to remain in this city. It is best if Monsieur Manette is out of France."

In the submissive way of one long accustomed to obey, Dr Manette ate and drank what they gave him, and put on the cloak they had brought. Taking his daughter's hand in his, Dr Manette followed her down the staircase to the courtyard below.

There was no one in the tiny courtyard, and no one to be seen in the street. Only one soul was to be seen, and that was Madame Defarge —who leaned against a door-post, knitting.

"Adieu," called Defarge as the postilion cracked his whip and the coach clattered away down the cobbled street.

2 Acquitted

Five years passed. On a windy morning in March, in the year 1780, Jerry Cruncher, messenger of Tellson's bank, London, left his lodgings in Whitefriars. By eight forty-five he had taken up his station outside the bank in Temple Bar.

"Messenger wanted!" called a voice from inside the bank. "Take this note to Mr Lorry at the Old Bailey?"

"In the court, sir?"

"In the court. And wait there. Mr Lorry wishes to have a messenger at hand."

Jerry took the letter and made his way through the city until he came to the doors of the Old Bailey. After some delay a door grudgingly opened and allowed Jerry to squeeze himself into the court. There he handed the note to a clerk of the court, who took it to Mr Lorry who was seated at a table, among the gentlemen in wigs, one of whom sat with his hands in his pockets, staring up at the ceiling.

"What's on?" asked Jerry of the clerk when he returned.

"Treason case."

"The hanging and quartering one, eh?"

The entrance of the judge and then a great stir and settling down in court, stopped the dialogue. Two gaolers, who had been standing by the dock, went out and brought the prisoner.

Everyone present, except a lawyer named Sydey Carton, who looked at the ceiling, stared at him; eager faces strained round pillars and corners, to get a sight of him; spectators in back rows stood up, not to miss a hair of him. And object of all this staring was a tall, good-looking young man of about twenty-five.

"Silence in the court! Mr Attorney-General, please read the indictment against the prisoner,

Charles Darnay."

"The prisoner is charged with treason against our most serene, illustrious, lord King George III, in that he has passed to agents of the French King Louis, secret information listing the strength of the forces that His Majesty had intended to send to America." The accused neither flinched or changed his expression. He was quiet and attentive, watching the proceedings with a grave interest, and standing with his hands resting on the bar of the dock.

"The Crown seeks to prove the case against Charles Darnay," continued the Attorney-General, "with the evidence we now lay before the court. Call John Barsad."

Mr Solicitor-General then, following his colleague's lead, questioned John Barsad.

"John Barsad, you are acquainted with Mr Darnay, are you not?"

"Yes, sir."

"And is it not true that you followed your patriotic duty when you saw the prisoner to be in possession of secret lists indicating troop movements?"

"That is true, sir. I felt it my duty to report it to your office."

"And did you not see the prisoner hand these same lists to French gentlemen both at Calais and Boulogne?"

"Yes, sir, I did."

"Thank you, Mr Barsad, you have acted like a patriot. Your witness, Mr Stryver."

Mr Solicitor-General sat down with a look of satisfaction. Mr Stryver, the prisoner's counsel, then rose. "Mr Barsad, have you ever been a spy?"

"No, sir."

"Is it not true that you have been in a debtor's prison, not once or even twice, but six times?"

"Well — yes."

"And that you have borrowed money from my client, money which you have not repaid?"

"No! Not true!"

"Furthermore, your acquaintance with Mr Darnay is, in fact, very slight, is it not, forced upon him by you?"

"No."

"I put it to you, Mr Barsad, that you have fabricated your entire story in order to gain money, and that you are, in fact, a government informer, paid to lay traps!"

A buzz arose in the court as if a cloud of blue-flies were swarming about the prisoner.

"No! No!" pleaded Barsad. "It's not true. It isn't!"

When John Barsad had stood down, Roger Cly was called to the stand. Briefly, Cly stated that he had been engaged by the prisoner as man-servant, but that he began to have suspicions about the prisoner which were later confirmed when he saw in the drawer of the prisoner's desk lists such as those shown to the court by the Attorney-General.

Under cross-examination, he also admitted that he had known the previous witness, John Barsad, for a period of some eight years. But he denied, emphatically, Mr Stryver's suggestion that he and Barsad were in collusion in order to extract money from the prisoner. True patriotism was his only motive.

Mr Jarvis Lorry was then called to the witness stand.

"Mr Lorry, on a certain Friday night in November 1775 did business occasion you to travel between London and Dover by coach?"

"It did."

"Mr Lorry, look at the prisoner. Was he one of two other passengers in the coach?"

"I cannot say that he was," replied Mr Lorry. "Both passengers were well wrapped against the cold. And the night was so dark that I did not see their faces."

"Look once more at the prisoner. Have you seen him before, to your certain knowledge?"

"I have. I was returning from France a few days later, and at Calais the prisoner came on board the packet-ship in which I returned, and made the voyage with me."

"Were you travelling alone, Mr Lorry."

"I was in the company of Dr Manette and his daughter."

"Did you speak to the prisoner during the voyage?"

"Hardly at all. The crossing was rough and I spent most of the time in my cabin."

"Thank you, Mr Lorry, that is all Call Miss Lucie Manette!"

The young lady, to whom all eyes now turned, stood up. Her father rose with her and kept her hand drawn through his arm.

"Miss Manette, have you seen the prisoner before?"

"Yes, sir. On board the packet-ship just now referred to."

"Miss Manette, did the prisoner come on board, alone?"

"No, sir, he was accompanied by two French gentlemen."

"Will you please tell the court about the conversation I believe you had with the prisoner, Miss Manette."

"When the prisoner came on board he noticed that my father was in a very weak state of health, and offered to assist me in finding him shelter, away from the wind and rain. He expressed great gentleness and kindness for my father's condition and I am sure he felt it. I hope, sir, I may not repay him by doing him harm, today."

"Miss Manette, I am sure that the prisoner understands that you must tell the truth. Please continue."

"He — he told me he was on business of a delicate nature, that might get people into

trouble, and that he was therefore travelling under an assumed name."

"Did the prisoner say anything about America, Miss Manete. Be particular."

"He spoke of England's quarrel with America and said that it was a wrong and foolish one on England's part. He added, in a jesting way, that perhaps George Washington might one day be as famous as King George the Third."

After the judge had looked up to glare at the heresy about George Washington, Mr Attorney-General continued his case by explaining to the court that the prisoner had gone down with some fellow-plotter in the Dover Mail that Friday night five years before and had then travelled to a garrison and dockyard where he collected information. This information was subsequently handed to the French; a witness was then called who claimed to have seen the prisoner in the coffee-room of an hotel in the garrison-and-dockyard town, at the precise time required, meeting another person.

Mr Stryver was cross-examining this witness when the wigged gentleman who had all this time been looking at the ceiling, wrote a word or two on a piece of paper, screwed it up, and tossed it at Mr Stryver. Opening the piece of paper, Mr Stryver looked with great attention at the prisoner.

"You say again that you are quite sure that it *was* the prisoner?"

"Quite sure," replied the witness.

"Did you ever see anybody very like the prisoner?"

"Not so like as I could be mistaken."

"Look well upon that gentleman, my learned friend there," he said, pointing to him who had tossed the paper over, "and then look well upon the prisoner. How say you? Are they not very like each other?"

They were, in fact, so like each other to surprise, not only the witness, but everybody present. And when the judge asked Sydney Carton (my learned friend's name) to remove his wig, the likeness was even more remarkable.

In a voice that seemed to threaten doom, the Judge turned to the jury and said, "We have heard the testimony of over twenty witnesses. The Attorney-General has put forward a case which relies too much, in my opinion, on circumstance, supposition, and suspect witnesses. And in view of the remarkable resemblance the prisoner bears to my learned friend Mr Carton, I wonder whether it is he who we should really be trying for treason.

"You must ponder this case carefully. An ill-considered verdict could send an innocent man to a terrible death. On the other hand, if you are convinced the charges are fully proven, you must find the prisoner guilty. You will now retire to consider the evidence."

An hour and a half limped heavily by before the jury returned.

"Jerry! Jerry!" called Mr Lorry when the jury had returned and given their verdict.

"Here, sir! Here I am, sir!"

Mr Lorry handed him a piece of paper. "Quick! Have you got it?"

"Yes, sir!"

Hastily written on the paper was the word "ACQUITTED".

"If you had sent the message, 'Recalled to Life,' " muttered Jerry, "I should have known what you meant, this time!"

3 The Golden Thread

In a dimly-lit passage outside the courtroom, Mr Stryver stood congratulating his client — just released — on his escape from death, with Mr Lorry, Dr Manette and his daughter. Charles Darnay kissed Miss Manette's hand fervantly, then turning to Mr Stryver, thanked him warmly.

Only Sydney Carton, to whom the prisoner owed his life more than to any one else, was absent. He stood leaning against the wall where the shadow was darkest, unseen. But when the group finally dispersed, he followed Charles Darnay out of the Old Bailey and stopping him on the pavement, said, "Do you not think, Mr Darnay, that it is strange that fate should have thrown us together?"

"To tell the truth, Mr Carton, the events of today have been so extraordinary, I hardly seem yet to belong to this world at all."

"I don't wonder at it. But come, let me show you to the nearest tavern."

To this Charles Darnay agreed and after a good, plain dinner, Carton, who had been drinking steadily and had eaten nothing, looked at his companion full in the face and said, "Do you now feel that you belong to the world again, Mr Darnay?"

"I'm still rather confused, but I think so."

"It must be an immense satisfaction to you," said Carton bitterly. "As to me, the greatest desire I have is to forget that I do belong to it. It has no good in it for me, nor I for it. So we are not much alike in that particular. Indeed, I begin to think we are not much alike in any particular, you and I."

Charles Darnay, at a loss to know what to say, said nothing.

"Now your dinner is done," said Carton, filling their glasses again, "why don't you give your toast?"

"What toast?"

"The toast that's on the tip of your tongue!"

"Miss Manette, then!"

"Miss Manette, then!"

"That's a fair young lady to be pitied by. How does it feel? Is it worth being tried for one's life to be the object of such sympathy and compassion, Mr Darnay?"

Again Darnay answered not a word.

"Do you think I like you, Mr Darnay?"

"Really, Mr Carton! I have not asked myself the question."

"Then ask yourself the question now."

"You have acted as if you do; but I don't think you do."

"A last word Mr Darnay: do you think that I am drunk?"

"I think that you have been drinking."

"And you shall know why. I care for no man on earth and no man on earth cares for me."

"Much to be regretted. You might have used your talents better." And with that Darnay paid his bill and left.

As soon as Darnay had gone, Carton took up the candle, went over to a mirror that hung on the wall, and surveyed himself closely in it.

"Why don't you like the man who resembles you?" he asked himself. "Because he shows you what you might have been! Change places with him and you would have been looked at by those beautiful eyes in court today as he was. Come now, in plain words, admit it — you hate him."

As the months rolled by, Charles Darnay became a frequent visitor to Dr Manette's quiet house, not far from Soho Square. And with the passage of time his love for Lucie deepened, as did her love for him, though neither of them spoke of it to the other.

And though Dr Manette liked and admired Charles, he seemed sometimes to be very worried. If he thought anything of his long and bitter imprisonment, he never shared his thoughts with anyone. Those years and the fate of France, his homeland, were never mentioned.

Sydney Carton, together with Mr Lorry, were also frequent visitors. Mr Lorry, ever patient, thoughtful and jovial; Sydney Carton, always quiet and morose. If ever he shone anywhere, he certainly never shone in the house of Dr Manette. On Sunday afternoons he would join Dr Manette, Mr Lorry, Lucie and Darnay under the old plane tree in the garden and listen to the footsteps of passers-by. On one such afternoon, hot and oppressive, with the threat of a storm in the air, Lucie said,

"Sometimes, I have sat here alone listening to the echo of the footsteps in the street, and imagined them to be the footsteps of all the people coming into our lives."

"Then there is a great crowd coming into our lives, one day, Miss Manette," answered Sydney Carton.

No one knew, least of all him, how true his words were soon to prove.

4 The Storm Gathers

While life in London for Dr Manette and his daughter passed quietly and happily, the lives of the common people of Paris grew steadily worse.

Typical of the hated aristocracy was Monsieur the Marquis d'Evrémonde, a man of about sixty, expensively dressed and haughty in manner. When driving in Paris, Monsieur the Marquis took pleasure in seeing the poor people disperse before the horses of his carriage, barely escaping with their lives.

That same Sunday when Dr Manette and his daughter were sitting under the old plane tree, Monsieur the Marquis' carriage rattled and clattered through Paris, sweeping round corners, dashing through the streets. Women screamed and men clutched their children as the carriage swept on. At last, by a fountain in a cobbled street, it came to a sickening halt. There was a loud cry from a number of voices and the horses reared and plunged.

"What's wrong?" asked Monsieur, calmly looking down.

A tall man picked up a bundle from among the feet of the horses, and howling over it like a wild animal, laid it on the base of the fountain.

"Pardon, Monsieur the Marquis!" said a ragged and submissive man. "It is a child!"

"Why does he make that abominable noise? Is it his child?"

"Killed!" shrieked the man by the fountain, staring at the Marquis. "Dead!"

The people closed round, and looked at Monsieur the Marquis. There was no visible sign of anger, neither did they say anything. Monsieur the Marquis ran his eyes over them, as if they were rats come out of their holes. Then he took out his purse.

"It is extraordinary to me that you people cannot take care of yourselves and your children. One or the other of you is forever in the way. How do I know what injury you have done my horses? See! Give him that."

He threw a gold coin for his driver to pick up. All heads craned forward so all might see it as it fell. The tall man called out again with an unearthly cry, "Dead! Dead!"

He was held by another man, newly arrived on the scene, for whom the crowd made way. On seeing him, the miserable creature fell upon his shoulder, sobbing and crying, and pointing to the fountain, where some women were stooping over the motionless bundle.

"I know, I know," said the late comer. "Be brave, Gaspard, be brave. It is better for the poor little thing to die so, than to live. It has died in a moment without pain. Could it have lived an hour as happily?"

"You there, you're a philosopher," said the

Marquis throwing another gold coin, "spend it as you will. The horses, are they all right?"

Without deigning to look at the crowd a second time, Monsieur the Marquis leaned back in his seat, and was just being driven away when his ease was suddenly disturbed by a coin flying into his carriage and ringing on its floor.

"Hold!" said the Marquis. "Hold the horses! Who threw that?"

He looked at the spot where Defarge had stood, a moment before; but instead of Defarge, the wretched father was grovelling on his face on the pavement and the figure that stood beside him was that of a stout, dark woman, knitting.

"You dogs!" said the Marquis, smoothly. "I would ride over any one of you and exterminate you from the earth. If I knew which rascal threw at the carriage, and if he were sufficiently near it, he should be crushed under the wheels."

Not a voice, or a hand, or even an eye was raised. Among the men not one. But the woman who stood knitting looked up steadily, and looked the Marquis in the face. It was not for his dignity to notice it; his contemptuous eyes passed over her, and over all the other rats. Leaning back in his seat again he gave the word "Go on!"

Marquis, smiling. "What do they call you?"

"They call me Defarge."

"Of what trade?"

"Vendor of wine, Monsieur the Marquis."

"Pick that up, vendor of wine," said the

The château of Monsieur the Marquis had a large stone courtyard before it and two stone sweeps of staircase meeting in a stone terrace before the main door. A stony business altogether, with stone urns and stone flowers and stone faces of men and lions.

The great door clanged behind him, as Monsieur the Marquis crossed a grim hall. Avoiding the larger rooms, which were dark and locked for the night, the Marquis with his candle-bearer going on before, went up the staircase to a door in a corridor. This admitted him to his own private apartment of three rooms. In the third of the rooms was a supper-table laid for two. The Marquis sat down to a sumptuous and choice supper. Halfway through he stopped, hearing the sound of wheels.

"Ask who is arrived."

It was the nephew of Monsieur the Marquis; known in England as Charles Darnay.

Monsieur the Marquis greeted his nephew in a courtly manner, but they did not shake hands. So long as a servant was present no words passed between them. But after coffee had been served and they were alone, the nephew said, "I have come back to tell you that this property and France are lost to me, and that I renounce them."

The Marquis took a gentle pinch of snuff from his box and shook his head. "Are they yours to renounce? I merely inquire. France may be, but is the property? It is scarcely worth mentioning, but is it?"

"I had no intention, in the words I used, to claim it yet. I just wished you to know that when it passes to me from you — tomorrow or twenty years hence — I would abandon it, and live otherwise and elsewhere."

"Hah!" said the Marquis, glancing round the luxurious room in a well-satisfied manner.

"To the eye it is fair enough, perhaps, but in reality it is a crumbling tower of waste, mismanagement, extortion, debt, mortgage, oppression, hunger, and suffering."

"Hah!" said the Marquis again. "Forgive my curiosity, but how do you intend to live?"

"I must do what the majority of my countrymen do — work."

"In England?"

"Yes, in England. Don't worry, the family 'honour' is safe from me in this country."

"My friend, I will die, perpetuating the system under which I have lived." And with that the Marquis rang the bell. "Goodnight, Charles. I look to the pleasure of seeing you again in the morning. Light Monsieur my nephew to his chamber," he said, turning to the servant. "And burn Monsieur my nephew in his bed," he added to himself.

The next morning the sun shone on the great stone faces of the château. One more stone face had been added overnight — the stone face for which it had waited for over two hundred years. It lay on the pillow on Monsieur the Marquis. Driven home into the heart of the stone figure attached to it, was a knife. Round its hilt was a frill of paper, on which was scrawled:

Drive him fast to his tomb. This from Jacques.

5 Two Promises

It was again a summer day when, lately arrived in London from France, Charles Darnay turned into the quiet corner in Soho, bent on seeking an opportunity of speaking to Dr Manette alone.

The doctor was reading in his armchair when Darnay entered.

"Charles! I rejoice to see you. We have been counting on your return these past three or four days. Mr Stryver and Mr Carton were both here yesterday, and both said you were due."

"I'm obliged to them for their interest in the matter. Miss Manette is —"

"Well," said the Doctor, "and your return will delight us all."

"Dr Manette, I knew she would not be at home. I took the opportunity to beg to speak with you alone."

"Is Lucie the subject?"

"She is. Dr Manette, I love your daughter devotedly. If ever there were love in the world, I love her."

The Doctor turned his face away, and his eyes looked on the floor. "Have you any reason to suppose that Lucie loves you?"

"None — as yet, none. And I know that without your approval, I could have no hope."

"If Lucie should ever tell me that you are essential to her perfect happiness, I will give her to you."

"Thank you, Dr Manette. Your confidence in me ought to be returned with full confidence on my part. My present name, though but slightly changed from my mother's, is not my own. I wish to tell you what that is, and why I am in England."

"Stop! Stop!" For an instant the Doctor had his two hands at his ears; for another instant he even had his two hands on Darnay's lips.

"Tell me when I ask you, not now. If your

attentions should prosper, if Lucie should love you, you shall tell me on the morning of your marriage. Do you promise?"

"Willingly."

"Give me your hand. She will be home directly and it is better she should not see us together. Go! And God bless you!"

A few days later, Sydney Carton's footsteps took him to the Doctor's house. He was shown into the garden, where he found Lucie alone.

"I fear you are not well, Mr Carton!"

"No. But the life I lead, Miss Manette, is not conducive to good health."

Looking gently at him again, she was surprised and saddened to see that there were tears in his eyes. There were tears in his voice too, when he said, "Don't be afraid to hear me. Don't shrink from anything I say. I am like one who died young."

"No, no, Mr Carton! I am sure that the best part of it might still be."

He shook his head. "Do not distress yourself, Miss Manette. There is just one thing I wish you to know. For you, and for any dear to you, I would do anything. Try to hold in your mind this one thing: that there is a man who would embrace any sacrifice — give his life, to keep a life you love beside you!"

He said "Farewell!", a last "God bless you!" and was gone.

To the eyes of Jeremiah Cruncher, sitting on his stool outside Tellson's bank the next day, the funeral procession pouring down Fleet Street presented an unusual attraction. Jerry always pricked up his senses and became excited when a funeral procession passed by, and today was no exception.

Having discovered that it was bound for the old church of Saint Pancras, far off in the fields, Jerry joined in the procession of mourners, and remained with it until the body had been interred. The dead man disposed of to Jerry's satisfaction, he went home to tea.

"You going out tonight, Jerry?" asked his wife.

"Yes I am, what's it to you?"

"May I go with you, father?" asked Young Jerry.

"No, you mayn't. I'm a-going — as your dear mother knows — a fishing. That's where I'm a-going. Going fishing. But I ain't going out till you've been long a-bed."

The evening wore away with the Cruncher family until Young Jerry, and his mother, were ordered upstairs. Mr Cruncher then sat down and smoked his pipe. It was not until the ghostly hour of one o'clock that he rose from his chair, took a key out of his pocket, opened a locked cupboard and took out a sack, a crowbar, a length of rope and chain, and other items of fishing tackle. Then, having extinguished the light, Mr Cruncher went out.

Young Jerry, who had only pretended to have undressed when he went to bed, was not long after his father. Under cover of the darkness he followed him down the road and out into the street. Keeping as close to house fronts, walls

gravestones — it was a large churchyard that they were in — looking on like ghosts in white, while the church tower looked down on him like the ghost of a monstrous giant. The three men did not creep far before they stopped and stood upright. And they then began to fish.

They fished with a spade at first. And they worked hard until the awful striking of the church clock so terrified Young Jerry that he made off. But his wish to know more about his father's body snatching adventures, not only stopped him running away, but lured him back again. Peeping in at the gate a second time, he saw the three figures bent as if strained by a weight. Slowly they lifted the weight to the surface. Young Jerry knew very well that it was a coffin but, when he saw it, and saw his father about to wrench it open, he was so frightened that he made off again, and never stopped until he had ran all the way home.

and doorways, as he could, he followed his father for over half an hour, until he saw him stop and nimbly climb over a wall. Dropping softly on the ground he seemed to lie there a moment — listening.

It was now Young Jerry's turn to approach the wall; which he did, holding his breath. Crouching down in a corner he saw three men creeping through the grass and all the

From his father's surly manner the next morning, Jerry realized that something had gone wrong the night before. And when he asked his father why there was no fish for breakfast, he received a box on the ears by way of reply. In this happy mood Jerry Cruncher set off, as usual, for Tellson's bank.

6 Knitting

There had been earlier drinking than usual in the wine-shop of Monsieur Defarge, though there was more brooding than drinking; for, many men had listened and whispered and slunk about there who could not have laid a piece of money on the counter to save their souls.

It was about noon when a mender of roads entered the wine-shop. Madame Defarge set a glass of wine before him and from his shirt he took some coarse dark bread and sat munching and drinking.

"Have you finished, friend?" asked Monsieur Defarge in due course.

"Yes, thank you."

He beckoned to three men sitting in the shop, "Jacques One, Jacques Two, Jacques Three! This is the man I, Jacques Four, invited. Speak, Jacques Five!"

"You remember Gaspard," began the mender of roads, "whose child was killed by the Marquis?" All four men nodded. "He was taken away by six soldiers with his hands tied up behind his back. They drove him with the butt-ends of their muskets and beat him until his face bled. Then they took him to the prison and put him in an iron cage like an animal . . ."

"Go on, Jacques," said Defarge.

"There he remained for some days. Then, on a Sunday night, soldiers come winding down from the prison, their guns ringing on the stones of the street. Workmen dig, workmen hammer, soldiers laugh and sing. In the morning, by the fountain where the child was killed, they raise a gallows forty feet high. At midday a roll of drums and Gaspard is marched out of the prison, bound as before, with a gag in his mouth. He is hanged there, forty feet above the fountain and left hanging for days. . ."

"You have acted and recounted faithfully," said Defarge.

"How say you, Jacques?" demanded Number One. "To be registered?"

"To be registered, as doomed to destruction," replied Defarge.

"The château and all his descendents?" asked Jacques Three in a croaky voice.

"The château and all his descendents," repeated Defarge, grimly. "Extermination. Their names will go onto Madame's Defarge's

knitted register. In her own stitches and in her own symbols, which only she can read, are the names of all those whose crimes against the people of France will one day be punished. The name Evrémonde will join all the rest — and will never be forgotten. One day they will all be exterminated!"

Later that night, alone in the wine-shop, Madame Defarge spoke to her husband.

"What did Jacques of the police say to you?"

"Very little tonight, but all he knows. There is a spy planted in the area."

"Well!" said Madame Defarge. "I will have to register him. What do they call him?"

"He's English."

"So much the better. Name?"

"Barsad."

"Barsad, good! Christian name?"

"John."

"John Barsad," repeated madame. "Appearance?"

"Brown hair, dark eyes, height about five feet nine, long, thin, sallow face, expression, sinister."

"Oh my!" cried madame, laughing. "It's a portrait. He'll be registered tomorrow."

Next noontide saw Madame Defarge in her usual place in the wine-shop, knitting intensely. A rose lay on the table beside her. A figure entering the shop threw a shadow on madame which she felt to be a new one. She laid her knitting down and pinned the rose in her cap before she looked at the figure.

It was curious. The moment Madame Defarge took up the rose, the customers stopped speaking and gradually began to leave.

"Good day, madame," said the newcomer.

"Good day, monsieur," said Madame Defarge out loud, then added to herself as she resumed her knitting: "Good day — brown hair, dark eyes, height about five feet nine, long, thin, sallow face, expression, sinister! Good day, one and all!"

"A glass of cognac and some cool fresh water, if you please, madame."

When madame had given him his order she sat down and resumed her knitting.

"— Here is my husband!" she said at length.

As Monsieur Defarge entered the shop, the spy saluted him by touching his hat and saying with a smile, "Good day, Jacques!"

Defarge stopped short and stared at him.

"Good day, Jacques!" the spy repeated.

"You are mistaken, monsieur. That is not my name. I am Ernest Defarge."

"It's all the same," said Barsad. "Monsieur Defarge," he continued after a pause, "you will be surprised to hear that I have the honour of knowing some interesting people associated with your name."

"Indeed!" said Defarge, with indifference.

"Yes, indeed. Dr Manette and his daughter."

"Yes?" said Defarge.

"Yes," said the spy sipping his drink, "Miss Manette is going to be married, soon. Not to an Englishman; but to one, who, like herself, is French by birth. It is a curious thing, but she's going to marry the nephew of Monsieur the Marquis d'Evrémonde; in other words, the present Marquis. But he lives unknown in England; he's no Marquis there. There he's Mr Charles Darnay — d'Aulnais was his mother's family name, you know."

"Can it be true?" said Defarge in a low voice, when the spy had left.

"As he said it, it's probably false. But it may be true."

"If it is, when the Revolution comes — I hope for her sake that destiny will keep her husband out of France."

"Her husband's destiny," said Madame Defarge with her usual composure, "will take him where he is to go, and will lead him to the end that is to end him. That is all I know."

7 Storm and Victory

Nine years were to pass before the event the Defarges' had so long plotted and planned for came to pass. Nine long years during which Charles and Lucie married and lived happily in Dr Manette's old house.

Some half-dozen times a year, perhaps, Sydney Carton visited them and sat through the evening listening to the echoing footsteps of the people outside. But in July 1789 there were other echoes too, that rumbled menacingly from a distance. And it was now that they began to have an awful sound, as of a great storm in France with a dreadful sea rising.

On a hot, wild, night in July, Mr Lorry called in at the corner house. Sitting with Charles in the drawing room he watched the lightning flash over London and listened to the distant roll of thunder.

"We have been so busy in the bank today," he said, "that we have not known which way to turn. There is such uneasiness in Paris that our customers over there are moving their money and valuables to England."

"That looks bad," replied Charles.

"I know that to be sure. But I'm determined not to be peevish after such a day. Come and take your place my dear," he continued as Lucie entered the room, "and let us sit and listen to the echoes about which you have a theory."

"Not a theory, Mr Lorry, just a fancy."

"A fancy then. They are very numerous and very loud, though, are they not, tonight? Listen to them!"

The next morning, July 14, broke sunny and warm. In the shabby suburb of Saint Antoine, the poor gathered to form one vast crowd. With one tremendous roar a forest of arms rose into the air, like the shrivelled branches of a tree. From each hand there waved a threatening weapon: iron bars, muskets, knives, pitchforks, even bricks and stones forced from walls with bleeding hands.

Like a whirlpool, the crowd surged forward to Monsieur Defarge's wine-shop. Then suddenly, Defarge himself appeared with his wife, carrying an axe instead of her usual knitting.

"Patriots and friends!" he roared. "We are ready! In the name of all the angels and the devils, forward to the Bastille!"

To the sound of bells and the beat of drums, twenty-five thousand people surged through the narrow streets of Paris. Wave upon wave, they forced their way forward and stormed the cold walls of the hated Bastille.

"Follow me, women!" cried Madame Defarge. "We can kill as well as the men when the place is taken!"

From the prison's eight great towers a volley

of musket fire suddenly engulfed the crowd. Almost at the same time came a loud succession of booms as the Bastille's cannon poured smoke and flame into the struggling mass. Row after row fell to the ground, but still the sea of bodies surged on.

"Forward, comrades!" cried Defarge. "Forward!"

Boom, smash and rattle — the attack raged for four fierce hours. Cannon, musket, fire and smoke; bodies fell, bells rang, drums rolled and the sound of the wounded crying for mercy filled the morning air.

For four fierce hours the sound of battle rolled through the air as the great sea of vengeance beat against the walls of the Bastille. Then, when almost too exhausted by their efforts and heavy losses to carry on, they saw a white flag fly from within the fortress. Everywhere was tumult, deafening noise and exultation.

"The prisoners!" shouted Jacques One.

"The records!" cried Jacques Two.

"The secret cells!" yelled Jacques Three.

"The torture cells! The prisoners!" joined in a thousand frantic voices.

With Defarge at their head, the crowd rushed across the drawbridge, bearing the prison officers with them.

"Take me to the North Tower, quick!" demanded Defarge. "One Hundred and Five!"

Through gloomy vaults, past hideous doors of dark dens, down steep, winding steps, the terrified warder led Defarge and Jacques Three to cell One Hundred and Five, North Tower.

"Hold the torch high," ordered Defarge when they reached the dreaded cell, "and pass it slowly along the walls." The man did as he was told.

"Stop! Look here! What's this?" Carved into the wall were the letters 'AM'.

"Alexandre Manette!" cried Defarge, moving his stubby finger along the wall. "And here he wrote 'a poor physician'. This is the place. You, Jacques Three, rip that bed open and search it thoroughly."

While Jacques Three was doing this, Defarge himself searched the fireplace and chimney. Some mortar and dust dropped down. Cautiously he slid his hands along the inside of the chimney stack. A loose brick moved. Nervously he removed it and found what he had been looking for: Doctor Manette's secret papers!

"Nothing in the wood and nothing in the straw, eh, Jacques?"

"Nothing."

Stooping to come out at the low-arched door, they left the warder in Dr Manette's old cell and

retraced their steps to the courtyard until they were in the raging flood of people once more.

"See, there's my husband," a voice called out.

Madame Defarge stood close to a grim-faced old officer dressed in grey. He too was borne along by the crowd until suddenly they stopped. At first the officer was struck from behind. Making no sound, he stumbled and fell as a torrent of stabs and blows bore down on him. Still Madame Defarge remained close by him, unmoved and unmoving. Then suddenly she became animated. When the old grey man fell dead to the ground, she put her foot on his neck, and with one swift blow cut off his head with her cruel axe.

Saint Antoine's blood was up and the blood of tyranny and domination by the iron hand was down, down under the heel of Madame Defarge on the steps of the Bastille where she had trodden on the body to steady it for mutilation.

The sea of black and threatening people; the sea of swaying shapes, voices of vengeance and faces hardened in the furnaces of suffering until the touch of pity could make no mark on them, surged forward.

Seven gory heads stuck on the railings outside the accursed fortress; seven prisoners released

from its cold, stone walls; some discovered letters and others memorials of prisoners dead, long ago; such were the rewards and such were the loudly echoing footsteps of Saint Antoine, heard in the streets of Paris on that day in mid-July 1789.

8 The Track of the Storm

In such risings of fire and terror, Mr Lorry sat at his desk in Tellson's bank, London, on a steaming afternoon in August. Charles Darnay stood talking with him in a low voice.

"You can have no idea, my dear Charles," Mr Lorry was saying, "of the difficulty with which our business in France is conducted and of the peril in which our books and papers are now in. It is imperative that I go to Paris and rescue these papers without delay."

"And you really go tonight, Mr Lorry? I admire your youthful spirit, sir."

"Tut! Nonsense, I do go tonight, for business has become too pressing to delay."

Just then a messenger entered the bank and gave Mr Lorry a letter. It was addressed to "Monsieur the Marquis St Evrémonde, c/o Tellson's Bank, London, England."

"But I know nobody of that name!" said Mr Lorry after a moments reflection.

Nervously, Darnay said, "I know the fellow," after Mr Lorry had showed him the letter.

"Do you, by Jupiter?" declared Mr Lorry. "Then perhaps you will have the goodness of delivering it to him."

Very ill at ease with himself, Charles Darnay made his way home, where he opened the letter in private and read it. It was from his uncle's old man-servant, Gabelle, informing the present Marquis Evrémonde, known as Charles Darnay, that he, Gabelle, had been seized by the citizen's army with great violence and indignity and brought to Paris where he was now held in the Abbaye prison.

Nor was this all: the Marquis' house had been destroyed — razed to the ground, and the only crime for which he, Gabelle, was imprisoned, he wrote, was that of being the loyal servant to the emigrant aristocrat, Charles Darnay. The letter ended with the plea, "For the love of Heaven and the honour of your noble name, I beg you, Monsieur the Marquis, to secure my release. My only fault is that I have been true to you. Oh, Monsieur, I pray that you may be true to me!"

The letter struck Charles deeply. He knew that his honour and duty required him to go to Paris and secure the release of Gabelle. Yet his home was now in England and the danger which he faced in France as an aristocrat, though it meant nothing to him, would inevitably affect the lives of his wife and daughter. Thus tormented, Charles Darnay, heretofore the Marquis St Evrémonde, paced the room, with a sense of oppression in his heart.

Finally, he decided that he must go to Paris. Thus resolved he returned to Tellson's bank to take leave of Mr Lorry, though he said nothing of his own decision to leave.

"I've delivered that letter," he said. "There's no written reply, but perhaps you will take a verbal one?"

"Of course," said Mr Lorry, taking up his pocket-book and pen.

"It is to Gabelle in the Abbaye prison. Simply say, 'Letter received and will come'."

"Very well! My love to Lucie, and to little Lucie," said Mr Lorry at parting, "take care of them till I return." So saying, he entered the awaiting carriage and left with Jerry Cruncher, who was to accompany him to Paris.

That night Charles sat up late, and wrote two letters. One was to Lucie, explaining why he had to go and why he thought that it involved little danger to himself; the other was to the Doctor asking him to look after Lucie and their dear child in his absence. To both he wrote that he would send them word of his safety immediately after his arrival.

The traveller fared slowly on his journey from London to Paris that summer of 1789. And Charles Darnay was stopped at every town-gate and village taxing-house between Calais and Paris. Nothing but the letter from Gabelle got him through. Then at the very gates of Paris he was escorted by three armed guards to the local revolutionary official.

"You are going to Paris under escort, emigrant," he said after Charles had shown him his papers.

"But, why? I'm here of my own choice!"

"Choice! Listen to him!" said the man. "You are an aristocrat and must be escorted — and must pay for it."

Charles could do nothing but comply. His escort consisted of two mounted men in red caps and tri-coloured cockades, armed with muskets and sabres, who rode on either side of him. They travelled through the night, and at daybreak arrived at the barrier outside Paris.

"Where are the papers of this prisoner?" demanded the man before whom Charles was taken. One of the escorts produced them from the inside of his cap and passed them to the man.

"I have a letter, citizen, that will explain my

mission —" began Charles.

"You can explain it to Citizen Defarge, in there," said the man roughly, pushing Charles into another room.

Defarge looked at Charles' papers, then looked up at him. "You live in England, Evrémonde?"

"Yes."

"Then you are under arrest and consigned to the prison of La Force."

"Under what law, and for what offence?"

"We have new laws, Evrémonde, and new offences, since you were last here. Under the new laws you are an illegal emigrant and forbidden to return."

"When were these new laws passed?"

"Four days ago, emigrant."

"But that was when I left England! I have done nothing. Am I to be imprisoned without any means of presenting my case?"

"You will see. Others have been similarly buried in worst prisons, before now,"

"All I ask is that you communicate to Mr Lorry of Tellson's bank in Paris and tell him that I've been thrown into the prison of La Force. Will you do that for me?"

"I will do," said Defarge, doggedly, "nothing for you. My duty is to my country and the People. I am the sworn enemy of you and your sort. I will do nothing for you."

Later that same night, Mr Jarvis Lorry sat before a cosy fire in his room above Tellson's bank, Saint Germain, Paris, when he heard the sound of the bell at the gate. A moment later his door opened and two figures rushed in.

"Lucie! Manette! Miss Pross!" he cried in amazement. "What's this? What's the matter? What's happened? What's brought you here?"

"O my dear friend! My husband!"

"Charles! What of him?"

"Here."

"Here — in Paris?"

"Has been for some days — three or four — I don't know how many — I can't collect my thoughts. He came here unknown to us. He was stopped at the barrier and sent to prison."

Mr Lorry uttered an irrepressible cry. Almost at the same moment, the bell at the gate rang again, and a loud sound of feet and voices came pouring into the court-yard.

"What's that noise?" asked Doctor Manette, turning towards the window.

"Don't look!" cried Mr Lorry. "Don't look out! Manette, for your life, don't touch the blind!"

The Doctor turned, with his hand on the blind and said, "My dear friend, I have a charmed life in this city. I have been a Bastille prisoner. There is no patriot in Paris — in France — who, knowing me to have been a prisoner in the Bastille, would touch me, except to overwhelm me with embraces. My old pain has given me a power that has brought us through the barrier, and gained us news of Charles. I knew it would be so; I knew that I could help Charles out of all danger; I told Lucie so. — But what is that noise?" His hand was again on the window.

"Don't look!" cried Mr Lorry, desperately. "No, Lucie, my dear, nor you!" he said putting his arm round her, and holding her. "Lucie, my child, you must leave your father and me alone for two minutes."

He kissed her and guided her into another room and locked the door. Then, hurrying back to the Doctor he opened the window and putting his hand on the Doctor's arm, looked out with him into the court-yard.

"They are," Mr Lorry whispered, glancing fearfully round at the locked room, "murdering the prisoners. If you are sure of what you say; if you really have the power you think you have — as I believe you have — make yourself known to these devils and go to La Force. It may be too late, but let it not be a minute later!"

9 The Knock on the Door

Doctor Manette did not return until the morning of the fourth day of his absence. To Mr Lorry the Doctor said that he had been taken through a dreadful scene of carnage to the prison of La Force. There he had found a self-appointed Tribunal sitting, before which prisoners were brought singly, and by which they were rapidly ordered to be put to death. Presented to this Tribunal he had announced himself by name and profession as having been for seventeen years a secret and unaccused prisoner in the Bastille. One of the Tribunal then rose and identified himself as Defarge.

Charles was alive. That at least he had discovered. But the Doctor had to admit that though he had tried hard and would never cease trying to get Charles released, or at least brought to trial, as yet he had been unsuccessful. There was nothing more he could do at present but keep trying and hope that his influence would secure Charles' release.

Throughout the following dark days and weeks Lucie was never sure from one hour to the next whether the guillotine had struck off her husband's head. Every day, the tumbrils jolted heavily through the streets, filled with the condemned: pretty young girls; bright women, brown-haired, black-haired and grey; men and boys, gentle born and peasant born; all red wine for the guillotine.

Sometimes, on kissing her father goodnight, Lucie would show the grief she had repressed all day. Calmly the Doctor always answered, "Nothing can happen to him without my knowledge. I know I can save him."

Weeks passed and still Charles remained imprisoned. Every day the Doctor visited him and pleaded with the Tribunal to release or at least bring him to trial. Yet nothing happened. Then one night when the Doctor returned home he said to Lucie, "My dear, there is an upper window in the prison to which Charles can sometimes gain access at three in the afternoon. When he can get to it — which depends of many uncertainties — he might see you in the street, he thinks, if you stood in a certain place that I can show you. But you will not be able to see him and even if you could, it would be unsafe to make any sign of recognition."

From that time, in all weathers, Lucie waited there two hours. As the clock struck two, she was there, and at four she turned away. On the third day of her going there, an old woodcutter, whom she had seen before, chopping logs in a clearing, greeted her.

"Good day, citizeness."

"Good day, citizen."

This was now the way the people of France addressed each other. It was the law for everyone.

"Walking here again, citizeness?"

"Yes, as you see," said Lucie coolly.

"Not that it's my business. My work is my business. See my axe. I call it my Little Guillotine. If those logs were aristocrats, I'd have France rid of them all within a week."

Then, raising his axe, he brought it down with a mighty blow saying, "And off his head comes!"

The log fell as he spoke. Lucie shuddered as he threw it into his basket.

Every day, the woodcutter was in the little clearing overlooking the prison of La Force.

And it was impossible for Lucie to stand there and not be seen by him. So to secure his good will, she always spoke to him first and often gave him money to buy a drink.

Charles saw Lucie — so she learned from her father who alone was permitted to visit him —

perhaps once or twice every five or six days. But it was enough for her to know that he could and did see her sometimes.

So the weeks and months rolled on until one wintry day, standing looking at the grim, old prison, she was joined by her father.

"My dear," he said, "I've just heard that Charles is to be tried tomorrow."

"Tomorrow!"

"Don't be afraid, my dear. I am well prepared and I know that I can secure his release. Now I must go and see Mr Lorry. Come, my child."

The court assembled early the next day. The Tribunal consisted of five judges, a public prosecutor and a jury. Fifteen prisoners were put in the dock before Charles Darnay's name was called. All fifteen were condemned and sentenced to death in the space of no more than an hour and a half.

At length "Charles Evrémonde, called Darnay," was called. The public prosecutor rose and accused Charles of being an emigrant, whose life was forfeit to the Republic under the

decree which banished all emigrants on pain of death. It was irrelevant, he said, that the decree was passed after Charles had returned to France. There he was, and there was the decree; he had been arrested in France and his head was demanded.

"Take off his head!" called out the crowd from the public gallery.

The President of the court rang his bell to silence them. Then, turning to Charles, he asked him whether it was true that he had lived many years in England.

It was, said Charles.

Was he not an emigrant then?

Not an emigrant, he replied, because he had voluntarily relinquished a title that was distasteful to him. Furthermore, he had lived by his own work in England as a teacher of French, rather than on the labour of the overburdened people of France.

What proof had he of this?

Two witnesses: Gabelle and Dr Alexandre Manette.

The mention of Dr Manette's name had a remarkable effect on the crowd and jury. Cries in praise of the well-known Doctor rent the hall.

Doctor Manette was next questioned. His popularity and the clearness of his answers made a great impression. Briefly he told the court that Charles Darnay was a long and trusted friend of his as well as being the devoted husband of his daughter Lucie; that he was a true friend of France and far from being in favour with the aristocratic government in England, he had been tried for his life by it as a foe, and that his motive in returning to France was to save a citizen's life. Was that criminal in the eyes of the Republic?

"No!" cried the crowd from the public gallery. Again the President rang his bell to quieten them.

The jury then declared that they had heard enough and were ready with their verdict. All were in favour of the prisoner being released. At this the President declared Charles Darnay free to go.

No sooner was the acquital pronounced, than Charles was embraced from all sides and placed in a great chair over which was draped a red flag and carried home shoulder high.

Having thanked the doctor for all his efforts in securing his release and Miss Pross for her devotion to Lucie throughout his long imprisonment, Charles greeted Mr Lorry, then took his wife in his arms.

Lucie could scarcely believe that he was really there. She had waited so long — but it was *not* another of the dreams in which he had come back: he really was there. Yet she trembled and felt a vague, but heavy, fear.

"What's that?" she asked, suddenly.

"Nothing, my dear," said her father. "You imagined you heard something."

"I thought I heard footsteps on the stairs."

A moment's pause, then there was a heavy knock on the door.

Startled, Lucie cried, "Who can it be? Quick, Charles, hide!"

"My dear," said Dr Manette rising and laying his hand on her shoulders. "What nonsense this is. Let me go to the door."

Taking the lamp from the table, he crossed the two intervening outer rooms and opened it. A rude clattering of feet over the floor and four rough men in red caps, armed with swords and pistols, entered the room.

"Citizen Evrémonde, called Darnay."

"Who seeks him?" answered Charles.

"I seek him. We seek him. I know you, Evrémonde; I saw you before the Tribunal today. You're under arrest."

"But why?"

"It is enough that you go straight to the prison of the Conciergerie. You are summoned for tomorrow."

At this the Doctor put down the lamp and confronting the speaker said, "You know him, you have said. Do you know me?"

"Yes, I know you, Citizen Doctor."

"Then will you answer *me*? Why has he been arrested?"

"Citizen Doctor," said the man, reluctantly, "he has been denounced to the Section of Saint Antoine. Ask no more. If the Republic demands sacrifices from you, without doubt you as a good patriot will be happy to make them. The People is supreme!"

"One word, please. Will you tell me who denounced him?"

"It's against the rules," answered the first; "but you can ask him of Saint Antoine here."

The Doctor turned his eyes to a man who moved uneasily on his feet. There was a pause before he said: "It's against the rules. But he's denounced — and gravely — by the Citizen and Citizeness Defarge. And by one other."

"What other?"

"Do *you* ask, Citizen Doctor?"

"Yes."

"Then you will be answered tomorrow. Now I am dumb!"

10 A Hand at Cards

Happily unaware of the new calamity at home, Miss Pross threaded her way along the narrow streets of Paris with Jerry Cruncher at her side. Crossing the river by the bridge of the Pont-Neuf they parted company; Mr Cruncher to buy wine and Miss Pross in pursuit of bread.

Having bought the wine, Jerry was leaving the little shop when he accidentally bumped into a man about to enter. "I know you, don't I?" said Jerry in amazement.

"What do you want" answered the man in a vexed, abrupt voice and in English.

"I never forget a face. I know — you was a spy-witness at the Old Bailey. Now, what was you called?"

"Barsad," said another voice.

"That's the name!" cried Jerry, turning to see who the voice belonged to. "Well blow me, what are you doing 'ere, Mr Carton?"

The speaker was indeed Sydney Carton. "You have a face to be remembered Mr Barsad," he said, "and I remember faces well. Seeing you coming out of the Conciergerie prison an hour or so ago roused my curiosity. So I followed you and gradually a plan shaped itself in my mind."

"What plan?" asked Barsad.

"These are desperate times," said Carton, "when desperate games are played for desperate

stakes. Now, the stake I have resolved to play for is a friend in the Conciergerie."

"You need have good cards," retorted Barsad.

"I'll run over them and see what I hold. John Barsad, spy and informer, now turnkey at the Conciergerie prison under a false name. That's a good card. Mr Barsad now in the employ of the republican French government, formerly in the employ of the aristocratic English government, the enemy of France and freedom. That's an excellent card. Perhaps Mr Barsad is still in the pay of the English government and is spying on the Republic. That's a card not to be beaten. Have you followed my hand, Mr Barsad?"

"Not to understand your game," replied the spy uneasily.

"Then I play my Ace. Denunciation of Mr Barsad to the nearest Section Committee. Look over *your* hand Mr Barsad and see what you have. Don't hurry."

It was an even poorer hand than Sydney Carton realized. As a spy for the overthrown French aristocratic government John Barsad had spied on Saint Antoine and Defarge's wine-shop. And he recalled with fear Madame Defarge knitting intently as he had spoken with her. He had since seen her in the Section of Saint Antoine, over and over again produce her knitted registers and denounce people whose lives the guillotine then swallowed up.

"You scarcely seem to like your hand," said Carton. "Perhaps you will when I reveal another

good card I have. That friend of yours and fellow turnkey at the Conciergerie, who is he?"

"French. You don't know him," said Barsad quickly.

"French, eh!" repeated Carton. "Well, he may be. Spoke good French, yet like a foreigner. And I'm sure I've seen him somewhere."

"I think not. I'm sure not. It can't be."

"Cly!" cried Carton. "That's who! Roger Cly! Disguised, but the same man as appeared at the Old Bailey with you."

"Nonsense" said Barsad, with a smile. "Cly's been dead for years; buried in London, at the church of Saint Pancras-in-the-Fields. I helped to lay him in his coffin, myself."

Just then, Jerry Cruncher, looking as if he had seen a ghost, tapped Barsad on the shoulder, and said, "Who took him out of it, then?"

"What do you mean?" stammered Barsad.

"I mean that you buried stones and earth in that there coffin. Don't go and tell *me* that you buried Cly. 'Cos me and two others know you didn't."

"How do you know?" asked the astonished Barsad.

"Yes, how *do* you know, Jerry?" asked an equally astonished Carton.

"Another time, sir," he replied, evasively, "the present time is inconvenient for explainin'. But I stand by wot I said. 'E knows well wot Cly was never in that there coffin."

"I see one thing," said Carton. "I hold another card, Mr Barsad. It's impossible for you to outlive denunciation when you are in communication with another aristocratic spy. A spy who, moreover, has feigned death and come to life again! Two foreign spies laying a plot in the prison against the Republic, eh? A strong card — a guillotine card, I should say. *Now*, do you play?"

"All right. I admit that I was a spy and that Cly is alive. We feigned the funeral because it was the only way he could get out of the country, though how this man knows it is a mystery to me. You said you had a proposal; what is it?"

"It would be dangerous to explain in the

43

"But access to him," said Mr Lorry, "will not save him."

"I never said it would."

Together, Mr Lorry and Sydney Carton left Tellson's bank; Mr Lorry to Dr Manette's and Sydney Carton to roam the streets. But he had not gone far when he stopped under a glimmering street lamp and wrote in pencil on a scrap of paper. Then, continuing his walk through the dark and dingy streets he came eventually to a chemist's shop. Entering, he handed the scrap of paper to a man who stood behind the counter.

The chemist whistled softly as he read it. "For you, citizen?"

"For me."

"You will be careful to keep them separate, citizen? You know the consequences of mixing them?"

"Perfectly."

Some small packets were made up and given to him. He put them, one by one, in the pocket of his coat, counted out the money for them, then left the shop.

street. Come, we will go to Tellson's bank. I have sad news to communicate to Mr Lorry. I will tell you of my plan on the way. Jerry, return to your home, but tell no one you have seen me. It's important that Miss Manette and her father do not know I am in Paris."

Mr Lorry had just finished dinner and was sitting before a cheery log fire when Carton entered his room. Sitting down in a chair he told Mr Lorry that Darnay had been arrested and taken to the Conciergerie prison. He then spoke of his meeting with John Barsad and Jerry Cruncher.

"But what do you hope to gain from this John Barsad?" Mr Lorry asked when he had finished.

"Not much," replied Carton casually. "If the verdict should go against Darnay tomorrow, I have ensured access to him, once."

Mr Lorry's countenance fell.

"It is all I could do," said Carton. "To propose too much would be to put Barsad's head under the guillotine, and, as he himself said, nothing worse could happen to him if he were denounced. It was obviously the weakness of my position."

11 Darkness

Returning to Tellson's bank the next morning Sydney Carton was told that Mr Lorry had already left for the court.

When Carton entered, the court was all astir and a-buzz. From an obscure corner among the crowd he could see Mr Lorry, together with Dr Manette and Lucie. The public prosecutor rose and delivered the indictment. Charles Evrémonde, called Darnay, was denounced as an enemy of the Republic.

The President of the court then asked by whom he had been denounced.

"Three people: I, Ernest Defarge, Thérèse Defarge, my wife, and Alexandre Manette, physician."

In the midst of the general uproar that then took place, Dr Manette, pale and trembling, rose to his feet. "I protest," he shouted above the crowd, "it's untrue. The accused, as you all know, is the husband of my daughter. I have

not, and would not, make any such accusation against him."

"Citizen Manette," replied the President, "if the Republic should demand of you the sacrifice of your child herself, you would have no duty

but to sacrifice her. Listen to what is to follow. In the meanwhile, be silent!"

Loud cheers greeted this rebuke. The President rang his bell and Dr Manette sat down. Ernest Defarge then stood up before the public prosecutor.

"You did good service at the taking of the Bastille, citizen?"

"I believe so, citizen."

"Inform the Tribunal of what you did that day within the Bastille, citizen."

"I knew that Dr Manette had been confined in a cell known as One Hundred and Five, North Tower. I was resolved that when the Bastille fell I would examine that cell. In a hole in the chimney, behind a loose stone, I found a written document. This is that written document," he said, waving it in the air. "I have made it my business to examine some specimens of the writings of Dr Manette. This is the writing of Dr Manette."

"Let it be read."

In a dead silence and stillness, the document was read.

I, Alexandre Manette, write this in my cell in the Bastille, during the last month of the year 1767. I write it at stolen intervals, under great difficulty.

One night in the third week of December 1757, I was walking on a quiet part of the quay by the Seine when a carriage, driven very fast, came up from behind me. Stopping, two men wrapped in cloaks got out.

"You are Dr Manette?" asked one.

"I am."

"Will you please enter the carriage?" As these words were spoken, both men moved so as to place me between themselves and the carriage door. They were armed. I was not. I could do nothing but comply.

We drove at great speed along a country road for some time. When we stopped, I was taken along a path to the door of a house, then up some stairs to a small room where a young woman of great beauty was lying on a bed. I was told that she had tried to take her own life. As the two men stood by the bedroom door I could see that they were of about my own age and that they looked very alike in stature, manner and face. From their appearance I guessed they were brothers.

"There are some medicines there," said one, pointing to a closet. "Do what you can."

I examined the patient immediately. Her breathing was so faint I could hear nothing. I felt her pulse. There was life, but no more. I could do nothing for her.

"There is another patient," said one of the brothers. I was taken to a loft over a stable. On some hay on the floor lay a peasant boy of not more than seventeen. Kneeling down I could see that he had received a deep sword-wound and that no skill could save him now.

"How has this been done, monsieur?" I asked one of the brothers.

"A crazed dog! A serf! He forced my brother to draw upon him," was the only answer I received.

But alone, the boy told me his story with his last breath. He was, he said, the brother of the young woman whom I had attended. She had been taken from their home by the younger brother for his pleasure and diversion. The boy had tracked them down and the previous evening had entered the house armed with a sword. But he had proved no match for the Marquis Evrémonde — for that, the boy revealed, was who the man was — and had been easily overpowered.

I did what little I could for the boy to make him comfortable, but he died soon after. And when I returned to the bedside of his sister it was not long before she died too.

When it was over the Marquis said, "The things that you have seen here are not to be spoken of, you understand?" He then offered me gold, but I said that I wanted no payment.

He looked at me curiously, but said no more. Then we parted.

The next day I wrote to the authorities stating all the circumstances of the two cases to which I had been summoned. I knew what immunities nobles enjoyed and expected to hear nothing more of it. But I wished to relieve my own mind. And not trusting the letter out of my own hands, I delivered it myself.

That night a man came to the house and said there was an urgent case in the Rue St Honoré and that he had a coach in waiting. Suspecting nothing, I got into the coach. But as soon as we were clear of the house a black scarf was drawn tightly over my mouth from behind and my arms were tied. We stopped and suddenly the two Evrémonde brothers appeared from across the road and identified me with a single gesture. The Marquis then took from his pocket the letter I had written, showed it me, burnt it in the light of a lantern that was held by the coachman, and extinguished the ashes with his boot. Not a word was spoken. I was then brought here to the Bastille, my living grave.

I, Alexandre Manette, unhappy prisoner, do this last night of the year 1767, denounce to the times when all these things shall be answered for, the Marquis Evrémonde, his brother and all their descendents, to the last of their race. I denounce them to Heaven and to earth.

As Monsieur Defarge finished reading the document, a terrible sound arose in the court, like a pack of hounds baying for blood. Swiftly and unanimously, the jury voted. Charles Evrémonde, at heart, and by descent, an Evrémonde still, a notorious oppressor of the People, was sentenced to death by guillotine within twenty-four hours!

When the court had dispersed and Lucie had said a last farewell to her husband, Sydney Carton paused in the street, undecided where to go. "Shall I," he thought to himself, "let those people know there is such a man as I here?"

Defarge had described himself, in the court that day, as the keeper of a wine-shop in Saint Antoine. It was not difficult for one who knew the city well to find his house. When Sydney Carton entered there was no other customer in the shop but Jacques Three and Madame Defarge's female companion known as The Vengeance. In broken French — though he spoke the language fluently — Carton asked madame for a little wine. He then took a seat close to the counter and pretended to look at a newspaper.

"English?" asked Madame Defarge, when she brought him his wine.

"Yes, madame, yes. I am English," he answered in a strong accent and with difficulty.

She looked at him carelessly at first, then closer and closer. She placed the wine on the table, then returned to the counter, looking as if she had seen a ghost. Carton heard her say, "I swear to you, just like Evrémonde!"

After a moment's silence, when all four at the counter had turned and looked at Carton, they continued their conversation.

"Extermination is a good doctrine, I agree," said Defarge, "but one must stop somewhere. Manette has suffered much already; you observed his face when the paper was read in court today."

"Yes, I observed his face," answered Madame Defarge. "I observed his face to be not the face of a true friend of the Republic. Let him take care of his face!"

"And you have observed the anguish of his daughter?"

"I have observed his daughter," repeated madame. "I have observed her today and on other days; in the court and in the street by the prison. Let me but lift my finger —." Carton felt her raise it, though he kept his eyes on the paper, and heard it fall on the counter, as if an axe had dropped.

"No! No!" protested Defarge. "I say let his death be the last."

"Then you forget, my husband," said Madame Defarge, "that night when the Bastille fell, how we read Manette's paper and how I said that I had a secret to communicate to you. Is it not so?"

"It is so," agreed Defarge.

"Then listen, Jacques Three and my little Vengeance, and I will tell you what I told him. That peasant family so injured by the two Evrémonde brothers, as that Bastille paper describes, is *my* family. That sister of that mortally wounded boy was *my* sister, that boy, *my* brother; those dead are *my* dead and the duty to answer for those things descends to *me*! Is that not so, Defarge?"

"It is so," answered her husband once more.

"Then tell wind and fire where to stop," replied madame, "but don't tell me."

Customers began to enter so the group broke up. Carton rose and paying for his wine, left.

At nine o'clock that evening he returned to Tellson's bank. Mr Lorry sat in his chair with his head bent low. "There's no hope," he said. "He will perish. Dr Manette can do nothing."

"Yes. He will perish: there is no real hope," echoed Carton. "But I come to warn you that Lucie is in great danger of denunciation by Madame Defarge. I know it from her own lips. And I have since seen Barsad who confirms it. He says that a wood-cutter, living by the prison wall, has been told by Madame Defarge to say that he has seen Lucie making signs and signals to prisoners. It's easy to see that she will say that Lucie is involved in a prison plot and that it will be her life that is at stake — perhaps that of her father as well, for he has been seen with her at that place. As you know, it is a capital crime to mourn for a victim of the guillotine. Lucie and her father would unquestionably be guilty of that crime. Madame Defarge will add it to her case to make doubly sure of their conviction. But don't look so horrified. *You* will save them."

"Heaven grant I may, Carton! But how?"

"I'm going to tell you how. It will depend on you and you alone. First," he said, putting his hand in his coat pocket and taking a paper from it, "this is the certificate that enables me to pass out of the city. Look at it. You see — Sydney Carton, Englishman?"

Mr Lorry held it in his open hand, looking at Carton's earnest face.

"Keep it for me until tomorrow. I see Darnay in prison tomorrow and I had better not take it with me."

"Why ever not?"

"I don't know; I just prefer not to do so. Now, take this and Dr Manette's certificate enabling him and his daughter to pass the barrier and the frontier, at any time. You follow me?"

"Attentively and with confidence in what you say," replied Mr Lorry.

"Good. Travel to the coast as quickly as the journey can be made. And so to England. Now, remember, have your horses and carriage ready in the courtyard here at two o'clock tomorrow afternoon."

"It shall be done."

"Tell Lucie tonight of the danger she is in, and impress upon her for the sake of her father the necessity of leaving Paris. Tell her it is her husband's last wish. The moment I come to you tomorrow, take me in and drive away. Promise me that nothing will influence you to alter the course on which we now stand pledged to one another."

"I promise, Carton."

"And remember these words tomorrow: change the course or delay it — for any reason — and no life can possibly be saved and many lives must inevitably be lost."

"I will remember them. I hope to do my part faithfully."

"And I hope to do mine. Now, good-bye!"

12 The Footsteps Die Out

In the prison of the Conciergerie, the doomed of the day awaited their fate. Fifty-two heads were to roll that afternoon. Charles Darnay, alone in his cell, heard the clock strike the hours he would never hear again. Nine, ten, eleven, twelve, all gone for ever. He wrote a long letter to Lucie and one to her father. Then, walking up and down the tiny prison cell, with his arms folded, he heard the clock strike one.

"There is but another now," he thought. Then he heard footsteps in the stone passage outside the door. He stopped. The key was put in the lock and turned. The door was quickly opened and closed. Before him stood Sydney Carton, face to face!

There was something so remarkable in his look that Darnay imagined it was an apparition before him. But the apparition spoke and took his hand. "Of all the people on this earth, you least expected to see me?" Carton said.

"I could not believe it to be you. I can scarcely believe it now. You are not — a prisoner?"

"No. I happen to know one of the keepers here, who agreed to let me in. I come from *her* — your wife. I bring you a request from her."

"What is it?"

"You have no time to ask me why I bring it, or what it means; I have no time to tell you. You must do what I say — take off those boots you wear, and put on these of mine."

Carton had already, with the speed of lightning, taken off his boots.

"Carton, there's no escaping from this place; it can never be done. You will only die with me. It's madness."

"It would be madness if I asked you to escape; but do I?"

"Now, there are pen and ink and paper on this

table. Write exactly what I speak," said Carton.

"To whom do I address it?"

"To no one," said Carton putting his hand in to his breast pocket.

"Do I date it?"

"No. *'If you remember,'* " said Carton dictating, " *'the words that passed between us, long ago, you will understand why I do this.'* Have you written it?" asked Carton.

"I have. Is that a weapon in your hand?"

"No; I am not armed."

"What is in your hand?"

"You shall know directly. Write on: there are but a few words more." He dictated again. " *'I am thankful that the time has come, when I can prove them. That I do so is no subject for regret or grief.'* " As he said these words with his eyes fixed on Darnay, Carton carefully took out a handkerchief from inside his coat and slowly and softly moved his hand down close to the writer's face.

The pen dropped from Darnay's fingers on to the table. Then he fell insensible on the floor. Quickly, Carton dressed himself in the clothes the prisoner had laid aside, combed back his hair and tied it in the ribbon the prisoner had worn. Then he softly called hurriedly, "Enter there!

Come in!" and Barsad presented himself.

"Take me to the coach." said Carton

"*You?*" asked Barsad, nervously.

"Him, man, *him* with whom I have exchanged. Take him to the courtyard of Tellson's bank, place him in the carriage, and tell Mr Lorry to remember my words and his promise of last night and drive away!"

The door closed and Carton was left alone.

Keys turned, doors clashed, footsteps passed along distant passages; no cry was raised, or hurry made. The clock struck two. Several doors were opened in quick succession and finally his own. A goaler, with a list in his hand, looked in. "Follow me, Evrémonde!" he said and Carton followed him into a large dark room.

Dimly he could see that others had been brought there to have their arms bound. Some were standing, some seated. As he stood by the wall in a corner, while some of the fifty-two were brought in after him, a young woman, with a slight girlish form, rose from the seat where he had seen her sitting, and came to speak to him.

"Citizen Evrémonde," she said, touching him with her cold hand. "Do you remember me? I was with you in La Force."

Carton murmured an answer.

"I am not afraid to die, Citizen Evrémonde. If I may ride with you, Citizen Evrémonde, will you let me hold your hand? I am not afraid to die, but I am little and weak, and it will give me more courage."

As she lifted her eyes to his face, he saw a

sudden doubt in them and then astonishment. He pressed her hand and raised it to his lips.

"Are you dying for him?" she whispered.

"And his wife. Hush! Yes."

"O you will let me hold your brave hand, stranger?"

"Hush! Yes, yes, my poor sister; to the last."

The same shadows that were beginning to fall on the prison that winter's afternoon were falling on the barrier when a coach from Paris drove up. Their papers examined, the coach drove on. When darkness fell Charles Darnay began to revive; to speak intelligibly. He feels a paper in his pocket, and thinks he is still in prison. The wind rushes past the coach and the clouds fly after it and it seems as if the whole wild night is in pursuit of it — but they are safe and pursued by nothing else.

In Paris the death-carts rumble. Six tumbrils roll along the streets. The crowds give out a cheer as they approach the guillotine. "Where's Evrémonde?" shouts someone in the crowd.

"There at the back, with his hand in the girl's," shouts out another.

"Down with Evrémonde. Death to all aristocrats! Down with Evrémonde!"

In front of the guillotine, seated in chairs are a number of women, busily knitting. The first tumbril begins to discharge its load. The executioners are ready and waiting. Crash! — A head is held up, and the knitting women who scarcely lifted their eyes to look at it a moment ago when it could think and speak, count One.

The second tumbril empties and moves on; the third comes up. Crash! — The knitting-women never faltering or pausing in their work, continue the count.

The supposed Evrémonde descends and the girl is lifted out next to him, still holding his hand. They stand with the other victims, composed, before the guillotine.

"But for you, dear stranger, I should not be so courageous. I think you were sent to me by Heaven."

"Or you to me," said Sydney Carton, gently. "Keep your eyes on me, dear child, and mind no other object."

"I mind nothing while I hold your hand. I shall mind nothing when I let it go, if they are swift."

"They will be swift. Fear not!"

"You comfort me so much! Am I to kiss you now? Is the moment come?"

"Yes."

She kisses his lips; he kisses hers; they bless each other. The spare hand does not tremble as he releases it. She goes next, before him — and is gone. The knitting women count twenty-two.

"I am the Resurrection and the Life, saith the Lord; he that believeth in me, though he were dead, yet shall he live: and whosoever liveth and believeth in me shall never die."

As Sydney Carton mounted the scaffold, he could hear the murmuring of many voices and see the upturning of many heads. The city, beautiful in the light of the dying day, lay spread out before him. Then, in a flash, everything passed away. Number twenty-three.

They said of him, about the city that night, that his was the peacefullest face ever beheld there; many added that he looked sublime, almost prophetic. As he mounted the steps of the scaffold, at the moment before the ugly axe fell, he was heard by those close by, to utter some last, sad, words,

"It is a far, far better thing that I do, than I have ever done; it is a far, far better rest that I go to than I have ever known."